MW01096839

THIS BOOK BELONGS TO:

_____

Copyright 2017 © Jane Brandi Johnson
All rights reserved.

No part of this publication may be reproduced,
stored in a retrieval system, transmitted in any form
or by any means, electronic, mechanical, photocopying,
recording, or otherwise, without prior written
permission of the publisher and author/illustrator.

Printed in the U.S.A. by CreateSpace, North Charleston, SC

Windermere's Wish
Authored by Jane Brandi Johnson
Graphic design and illustrations by Lisa Bohart
Pre-press production by Sven M. Dolling

ISBN-13: 978-1544862149
ISBN-10: 1544862148
Library of Congress Control Number:
BISAC: Juvenile Fiction / Imagination & Play

Printed in April 2017

Windermere's Wish

BY JANE BRANDI JOHNSON

ILLUSTRATED BY LISA BOHART

Hello! I'm back!
I'm off for a run— looking for fun—
chasing nuts and climbing the trees.

WOW!

What have I found, right here on the ground?

It's something I've never seen!

Hello, Windermere. I've come here to please.
I'll grant you ONE wish. So... what will it be?

POOF!

Well... I've bushels of nuts and a drey in a tree.
So, I'll ask for a wish— just special for me!

I want to...
take a long trip in a white limousine!

Play tennis at Wimbledon and visit the Queen!

Explore a jungle on an elephant's back,
while sipping my tea and munching a snack.

Fly with balloons up high in the sky,
through ice cream clouds and blueberry pie!

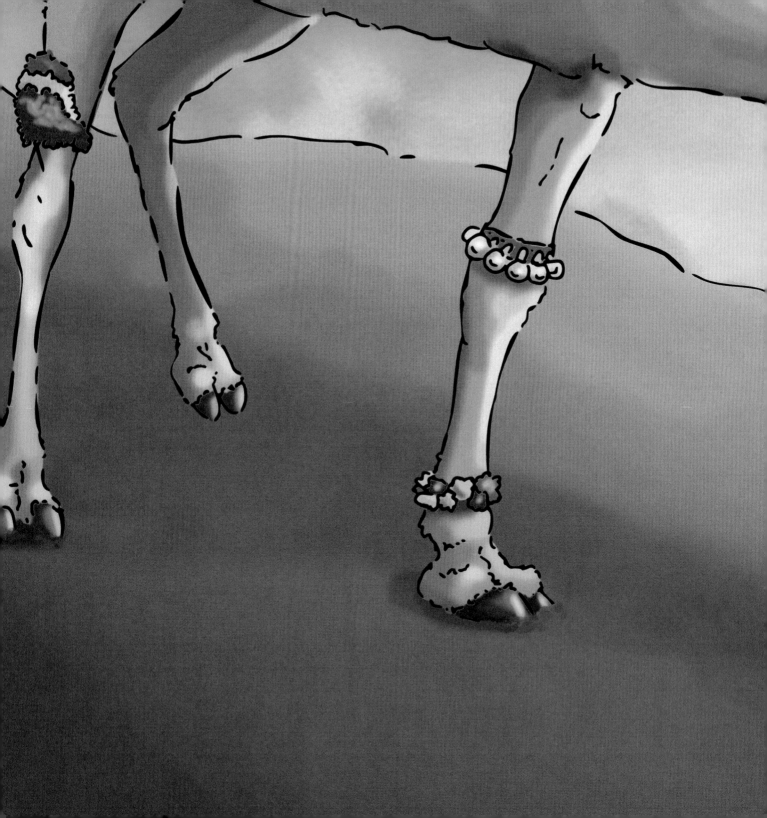

Ride a tall camel through hot desert sand,
tiptoeing into a faraway land...

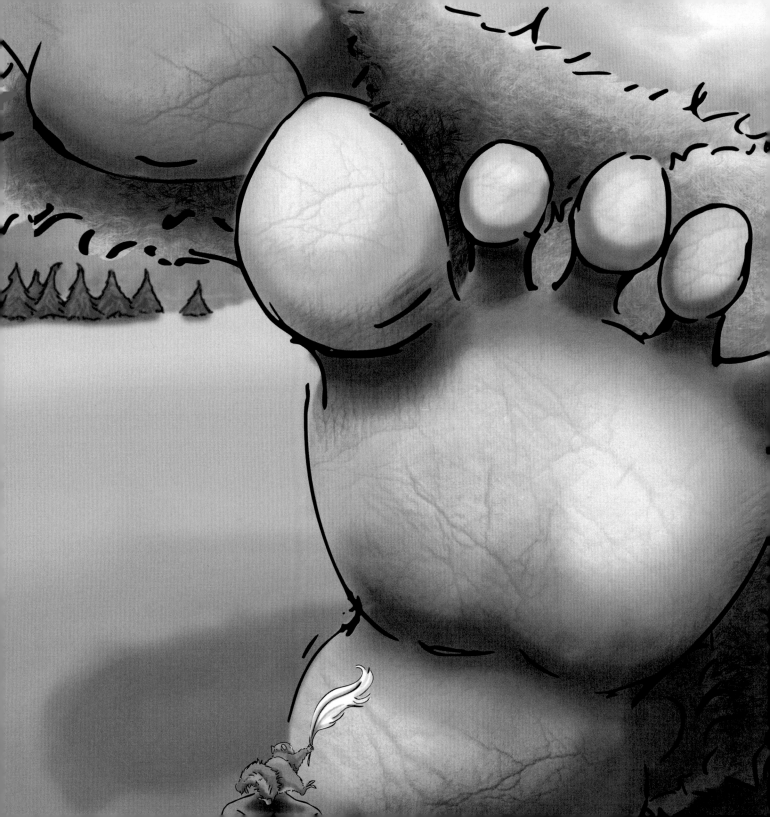

Tickle a giant as tall as a tree,
hiding myself— so he won't tickle me!

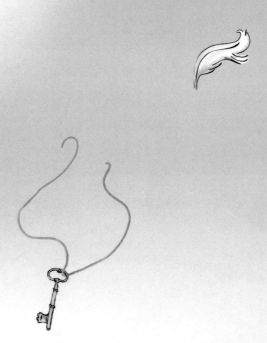

Open a door to a fiery dragon.
Then ride away fast—
in a fireproof wagon!

Paddle around in a tippy canoe,
avoiding the danger as best I can do.

Watch fireflies glow in the darkness of night,
as they dance for the King in their flickering light.

Dive with creatures in a deep blue sea—
until I find a BIG one— looking at me!

and, I want to...

STOP, Windermere!
Haven't you heard?
It's just one little wish—
ONE was the word!
You had only ONE wish.
Now you're making me SHOUT!
You've asked for too much—

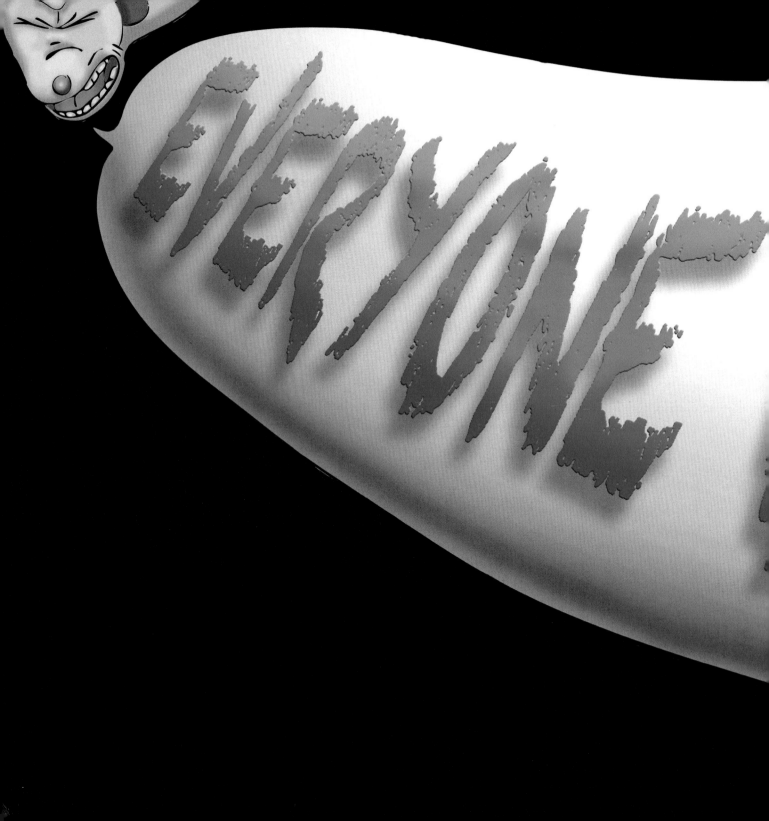

WAIT!
Don't take my wish! You'll just break my heart.
It's been only one wish— right from the start!
It's the best gift of all, and it's all that I need.
It's Windermere's Wish—

I just want to

Brilliant!

Your wish shall be granted!

48306328R00032

Made in the USA
San Bernardino, CA
23 April 2017